THE DINO FILES

Too Big to Hide

Stacy McAnulty

illustrations by Mike Boldt

A STEPPING STONE BOOK™
Random House 🏠 New York

Text copyright © 2016 by Stacy McAnulty
Cover art and interior illustrations copyright © 2016 by Mike Boldt

All rights reserved. Published in the United States by Random House
Children's Books, a division of Penguin Random House LLC, New York.

Random House and the colophon are registered trademarks and
A Stepping Stone Book and the colophon are trademarks of
Penguin Random House LLC.

Visit us on the Web!
SteppingStonesBooks.com
randomhousekids.com

Educators and librarians, for a variety of teaching tools, visit us at
RHTeachersLibrarians.com

The Library of Congress has cataloged the hardcover edition of this work
as follows:
McAnulty, Stacy.
Too big to hide / by Stacy McAnulty ; illustrated by Mike Boldt.
p. cm. — (The dino files ; # 2)
"A Stepping Stone Book."
Summary: Nine-year-old Frank, his cousin Sam, and cat Saurus's efforts to
keep Peanut the newly hatched dinosaur's existence a secret become more
complicated when their grandmother finds a new fossil that looks like
Peanut's horn, but a thousand times bigger, and a crew comes to make
a movie about it.
ISBN 978-0-553-52194-8 (trade) — ISBN 978-0-553-52195-5 (lib. bdg.) —
ISBN 978-0-553-52196-2 (ebook)
[1. Dinosaurs—Fiction. 2. Animals—Infancy—Fiction. 3. Fossils—Fiction.
4. Documentary films—Production and direction—Fiction. 5. Cousins—Fiction.
6. Paleontology—Fiction.] I. Boldt, Mike, illustrator. II. Title.
PZ7.M47825255To 2016 [Fic]—dc23 2015016996

ISBN 978-1-5247-0151-2 (pbk.)

Printed in the United States of America
10 9 8 7 6 5 4 3 2

This book has been officially leveled by using the
F&P Text Level Gradient™ Leveling System.

For Lily

CONTENTS

Dear Reader,

You look like a nice person. I think I can trust you. But just in case, I need you to take an oath before I let you read my story. Please raise your right hand and say:

I, (now say your name), promise not to tell anyone the TOP-SECRET story that is in this book. Not now and not ever. If I do spill Frank Mudd's secrets, may my teeth fall out and my tongue turn green.

Thank you. You're not going to believe what you're about to read. But trust me. It's all true.

Sincerely,
Frank Mudd
Future Paleontologist*

* All the dinosaur words can be found in my glossary.

A Thousand Times Bigger

Taking care of a dinosaur is hard work. That's why I like dinosaur naptime. It's when I get a break.

But not today. Just as my baby dinosaur, Peanut, falls asleep, Gram comes running into the house.

"Hot dog!" she yells. "You'll never guess what we found at the new dig site."

Peanut jumps up. He'll be cranky and tired later.

Gram should know better. She likes rules as much as I do. And one of my rules is: be quiet during dino naptime.

"What?" my cousin, Sam, shouts. She doesn't follow any rules.

"Is it another egg?" I ask. Gram found Peanut's egg a few weeks ago. I, Frank Mudd, was the one who sat <u>on</u> it and made it hatch. Well, me and my cat, Saurus.

"Nope," Gram says. "Think bigger!"

"Give us a hint, Dr. Mudd," Aaron says. He lives next door on a cattle ranch. Since Peanut came along, Aaron spends most of his time with us.

"You've got to see for yourself," Gram says.

Sam, Aaron, and I follow Gram to her truck. I have to bring Peanut with us. If we leave him home alone, he makes holes in things. Like magazines or blankets or walls.

I sit in the backseat between Aaron and Sam. We bug Gram with questions, but she won't answer any of them.

The truck stops in front of the fossil site.

My grandparents own the Dinosaur Education Center of Wyoming. Or DECoW, as we like to call it. Visitors can learn all about dinosaurs and even dig for fossils. Right now a family is visiting, and the dad is taking a video.

We leave Peanut in the truck with the windows open just a little bit.

"Please be good," I beg Peanut.

"You can kiss your steering wheel goodbye," Sam says to Gram.

We race to the pit. Aaron gets there first.

"Whoa!" he says.

"Is that what I think it is?" Sam asks.

"Wow!" I say.

At the far side is a giant fossil in the shape of a peanut. It's black and full of tiny cracks. But it's still in one huge piece.

"It looks like the horn on Peanut's snout," Aaron whispers.

"Exactly like it," Sam says. "Except a thousand times bigger."

"Not a thousand times bigger." Gram laughs. "Maybe a hundred times."

Peanut's horn is smaller than my pinky finger. This horn is longer than all of me.

The dad walks around with his camera.

"This is amazing," he says. "Brent, you probably made the dinosaur discovery of the century."

Probably not the discovery of the century, I think.

I look over at the truck, where a real dinosaur is locked inside. The truck shakes and rattles like a huge beast is trying to escape. Peanut is only fifteen pounds. He better learn some rules before he's bigger than a house.

"Excuse me," the dad calls to Gram.

"Yes." Gram puts on a fake smile.

"What kind of dinosaur is it?" he asks.

Sam jumps in front of the camera. "It's a *Wyomingasaurus*." Sam likes to jump in front of cameras. She thinks she's famous.

"Samantha." Gram gives her a warning look.

Sam talks into her plastic microphone. She never goes anywhere without it. "This is Sam McCarthy signing out."

"My son discovered a *Wyomingasaurus*." The dad gives us a big thumbs-up. "Brent, go sit on the fossil."

"No!" Gram and I yell.

"It's very fragile," she explains.

We wait for the family to take a million more pictures. I wish they would hurry. Peanut is squealing in the truck. Finally, they pack up their stuff and drive away.

"**That horn has** been here for over sixty-five million years," Gram says when we go back to the house for dinner. "It will be here tomorrow too."

The minute we walk in the door, PopPop calls us into the kitchen.

"You're going to want to see this," he says.

The small TV on the counter is on. Sam pushes me out of the way to get a look.

We all stare at the screen. I'm too shocked to talk. But not Sam.

"I'm famous!" she shouts. "I'm finally famous!"

Lots of Lettuce

The family's video from the dig site is on the local news. The picture mostly shows Brent and the peanut-shaped horn. You can see me and Gram in the background. Aaron walks by too.

"Look, there I am." Sam points at her elbow on the TV.

"Shhh." PopPop turns up the volume.

A pretty reporter shares the screen with

the video. "This footage was taken today at the Dinosaur Education Center of Wyoming in Starrville. It's the home of over a thousand dinosaur fossils, the most famous of which is Big Bob, the world's most complete *Super-saurus.* It was discovered here over thirty years ago. Could this giant fossil be Wyoming's next big dinosaur discovery?" The reporter raises her eyebrows.

Another reporter comes on the screen. He's sitting behind a desk.

"Thanks, Jennifer," the man says. "That is quite a fossil. Now let's turn to Weatherman Dave. He says we can expect some big storms over the next few days. Maybe even a threat of—"

ZAP!

Sparks fly from the back of the TV. The screen goes black.

Peanut yelps. He scrambles from behind the TV and out of the kitchen.

"He chewed the cord," Sam says. "Again."

I chase Peanut into the living room. When I bend down, he jumps into my arms.

"You can't eat wires," I tell him. "You could get hurt."

Peanut licks my face.

"You could get fried," Sam adds. "Then we'd have dino nuggets."

"Is he okay?" Gram asks.

"I think so." He could be brain damaged, but it's hard to tell because he's not that smart yet.

"We need to keep a close eye on him. He's going to destroy our home. Or worse, he could hurt himself." Gram crosses her arms.

I hold my breath, afraid she's going to say that Peanut doesn't belong in the house anymore. He's barely bigger than a cat right now. I'd like for him to stay inside until he's at least the size of a horse.

"Come on," PopPop says. "Dinner is getting cold."

I drop bits of lettuce and tomato on the floor for Peanut. PopPop keeps giving me a look. I'm not supposed to feed the dinosaur from the table for two reasons: Gram likes to write down everything Peanut eats, and it teaches Peanut bad manners.

We talk about the huge peanut fossil and how

our *own* Peanut will someday be big enough to ride.

"We certainly won't be able to hide him," PopPop says. "Planes will be able to spot him as they fly over."

"Will his habitat be big enough?" I ask. PopPop and Gram are donating some land. So are Aaron's parents.

"We have plenty of land," Gram says. "But we will still need money to build a fence."

"A big fence," PopPop adds.

"And Peanut will probably need a lot of food," Gram says. "Maybe as much as five hundred pounds a day. Taking care of a dinosaur won't be cheap."

I look at my plate. Five hundred pounds is a lot of lettuce.

"But that is not for you to worry about," PopPop says. "You and Sam are his herd. Just worry about being good family members."

. . .

The next few days at DECoW are the busiest I've ever seen. The TV news made it seem like it's easy to find a fossil from a newly discovered dinosaur. Now everyone wants one. People show up with shovels and even pickaxes. You don't use a pickax to dig for fossils.

There are visitors all over the place. We have to work extra hard to keep Peanut a secret. The list of people who know about him is small.

Me.

Sam.

Gram and PopPop.

Aaron Crabtree and his parents.

The vet who examined Peanut when he was sick.

And Saurus, my cat. But she doesn't speak English, so I totally trust her with all my secrets.

My parents don't even know yet. We live in North Carolina. That is where I go to school and keep most of my stuff. Wyoming is just my home in the summer.

Gram doesn't allow any more visitors at the site. I only get to go twice because Sam and I have to dino-sit Peanut. I'm better at it than Sam is. It's really like I'm dino-sitting Peanut and Sam.

Gram comes home to have lunch with us every day. She needs to eat, and she likes to make sure Sam and Peanut haven't broken any rules. But on Wednesday, Gram says she doesn't have time for lunch.

"Is everything okay?" I ask.

"Yes. PopPop wants me to talk to some folks," she says. "I won't be long."

"What's going on?" Sam asks.

"Boring DECoW business," she says as she heads for the door. "Stay in the house. I'll be back soon." Then Gram is gone.

"Stay in the house," Sam repeats. "Like that is going to happen."

Stark? Stark!

Sam and I fight over who needs to stay at the house and watch Peanut.

"I'm not responsible," Sam says. "You can't count on me to keep him safe. I'll probably feed him chocolate and let him play in traffic."

"Then just sit in the living room and don't feed him anything," I suggest.

Sam doesn't give in, and I don't give in. So we stuff Peanut in a backpack and head to DECoW.

The museum is full of visitors. We don't need to hide like spies. We are two ordinary kids walking around. I just happen to have a grumbling backpack.

We find Gram and PopPop in the office. The door is closed, but we can see in the window. They're talking to a man and a woman. A little girl with curly hair sits in the corner. The man has on a dirty blue baseball cap and holds a giant camera. It's the kind used by news crews.

Sam sees it too.

"That is a major, awesome camera," Sam says. "I bet they're here to do a talent search. Well, this is their lucky day."

Before I can stop her, she bursts through the office door.

"Is someone looking for a movie star?" she asks.

I roll my eyes.

PopPop shakes his head. "Mr. and Mrs. Stark, these are our grandchildren, Frank and Sam."

Stark? Stark!

"Are you Neil Stark?" I ask. The hair on my arms stands up.

"Yes." He smiles and touches the tip of his baseball cap.

I point at Mrs. Stark. "And you're Kristen."

She nods.

"I loved your documentary on the discovery of the *Oviraptor* nest in Mongolia. It was the best documentary on *Oviraptors* I've ever seen. And I've seen them all."

"A documentary is a movie, right?" Sam asks.

"Sort of. A documentary is true and it can be long or short," I explain. "The Starks do great dino documentaries. The best!"

Mrs. Stark shakes my hand. "It's always nice to meet a fan. This is our daughter, Mary."

"I'm five," Mary says, looking up from her book.

"Is she named after Mary Anning? The woman who discovered the first *Ichthyosaur* fossil?"

"Partly." Mrs. Stark laughs. "My grandmother was also called Mary. But I like Mary Anning too."

"I have to sit down." I take a seat on the ground and put my backpack next to me. This is one of the best days of my life.

"Why are you here?" Sam asks. She's still staring at the camera.

"We want to make a documentary about the dinosaur fossil your grandmother discovered," Mr. Stark says.

They explain that they saw the video on the Internet. The same video that was on the news. So they got in their RV—that stands for *recreational vehicle,* which is like a house on wheels—and drove all the way from California to check it out.

"This is great," Sam says. "I'll be the star of

your movie. I've got acting experience." She was in a commercial once when she was a baby.

"It's a documentary. There is no acting required," Mrs. Stark says. "I'm sorry."

"I'll be the host." Sam pulls her plastic microphone out of her pocket. "This is Sam McCarthy reporting from DECoW, where my amazing grandmother has made an amazing discovery—"

"Sam," Gram interrupts. "We haven't agreed to a documentary. It may be difficult to handle. We have a lot going on this summer." Gram pulls her lips into a tight line. She glances at my backpack.

I see Gram's point. It will be hard to hide a baby dinosaur with a film crew running around. But this is Neil and Kristen Stark. They love dinosaur fossils almost as much as I do.

"Maybe it wouldn't be so bad," I say.

"Dr. Mudd," Mr. Stark says, "this fossil is

unlike anything we've ever seen. It's amazing. Please let us make this documentary."

"We don't know if there are more fossils out there," Gram says. "This could be the only piece of the puzzle."

"That's the exciting part," Mrs. Stark says. "We never know what will be dug up."

Gram looks to PopPop. He shrugs. "It's up to you, dear." He kisses her cheek.

"Please, Gram," Sam says.

"Please, please, Gram," I say.

She lets out a deep breath. "I'm going to need some time to think about it."

And just then, Peanut lets out a loud cry. My backpack rolls across the office floor.

"Whoa," Mary says. "What's in there?"

It's a Cat

"**N**othing to see in that bag," Sam says. "Now, let's talk about my role in the movie."

The backpack flips onto its side. Mary jumps from her chair and moves closer. The bag groans. Mary should be scared. She's not.

"What is in there?" she asks again.

"Nothing." I pick it up.

"Is it a dinosaur?" Her eyes get big.

PopPop laughs. Gram laughs even louder. And the Starks laugh the loudest.

"It's my cat," I say, not laughing at all. "I better take him back to the house. I bet he wants to eat."

"It's just a cat," Mrs. Stark says. "A cat. Not a dinosaur."

"Remember, Mary, dinosaurs aren't real." Mr. Stark kneels down in front of her. "Well, they're not real anymore. They're extinct."

"X-stink," Mary repeats.

I say goodbye and go back to the house. Peanut is not happy. I can feel him chewing on the backpack's fabric.

When PopPop and Gram get home, they tell

us the good news. They're going to let the Starks make the documentary.

"We will make a bit of money," Gram explains. "It will help us build Peanut's habitat. I don't know how we'd pay for it otherwise."

"See?" PopPop says. "Things have a way of working out."

Sam and I give each other a high five.

"I'm going to be a movie star," Sam says.

"It's a documentary," I say.

"I'm going to be a documentary star!" she yells.

The next morning, I stay home with Peanut and Saurus so Sam can go to the dig site. After lunch, we'll switch and I'll get to go.

Saurus and Peanut don't like watching

documentaries as much as I do, so we go out-side to play.

A tall wooden fence surrounds the backyard. We can't see out, and no one can see in. That's a good thing when you're hiding a dinosaur.

Peanut runs around. He digs. He poops and pees. He eats the bushes. All normal dinosaur behavior.

I pick up a bright green Frisbee and throw it over his head.

"Fetch, Peanut." Peanut doesn't fetch because fetching is not normal dinosaur behavior.

"What do you guys want to do?" I ask Peanut and Saurus.

They don't answer. But another voice does.

"I see your dinosaur."

The voice is Mary's.

"It's a cat!" I yell.

"I see your cat too," she says. "He's cute."

I grab Peanut. "No dinosaur here!" I yell.

I open the back door and drop Peanut inside the kitchen.

He gives me an angry look.

"Where'd the dinosaur go?" Mary asks. I can see her eyeball through a small hole in the wooden fence.

I push the gate open.

"Hi," I say. "Do you want to see my cat?"

"I want to see your dinosaur." Mary walks into the backyard.

"There is no dinosaur. Just a cat."

"I saw a blue dinosaur," Mary says. "Or maybe he was green. He had a button on his nose."

"It was a toy. Do you want to hold my cat?" I shove Saurus at Mary.

"What's his name?" she asks.

"Saurus, and she's a girl cat. She came here with me from North Carolina. She's fluffy and sneaky and lazy. She's also my best friend."

"I like her name," Mary says.

I walk Mary over to the swings. She never lets go of Saurus. Mary is little, but I'm still worried that she could squeeze Saurus to death.

"She's a good kitty," Mary says. She sits down on a swing, with Saurus stuck in her lap.

"The best."

"Can I see the dinosaur now?" Mary will not give up.

"Sorry, Mary," I say. "Saurus is just named for a dinosaur. There is no dinosaur here."

Her face gets all scrunched up. I think she's going to cry. Then she smiles again.

"Do you want to see *my* dinosaur?" she asks.

Rapper

This kid is *crazy.* That is what I would have said before I found my *own* dinosaur.

"Is it a stuffed animal dinosaur?" I ask. I have forty-eight stuffed dinosaurs at home. I don't tell Mary that.

"My dinosaur is real. I'll show you." Mary looks down at Saurus. "But you can't bring your cat. My dinosaur might eat her."

Saurus jumps off Mary's lap and runs up a tree. Sometimes I think my cat *can* understand English.

"Fine," I say. "Let's go see your dinosaur."

"Okay," Mary says. "You have to promise to keep this a secret. Mommy and Daddy don't like to tell people."

"I promise." We seal the deal with a pinky shake.

I follow Mary to the Starks' RV, which is sitting in the DECoW parking lot. It's as long as a bus. That is still not a lot of room for a dinosaur.

Mary doesn't go into the RV. She goes to the trailer parked next to it. There is a horse painted on the trailer's side.

"He's in here." She pulls open the door.

Something growls.

"That doesn't sound like a horse," I say.

"It's not. It's a rapper." Mary waves me inside.

"A rapper?" I ask.

"Yep. Don't be afraid," Mary says.

"I'm not." *I am!*

It's dark inside the trailer. My eyes need to get used to no light. Then I see him, and he's awesome.

Mary's *rapper* is actually a *Velociraptor*. My knees shake because I know a lot about dinosaurs and science. *Velociraptors* eat meat, and I'm made of meat.

"This is Mike," Mary says proudly. "He is my dinosaur."

Mike the *Velociraptor* is the size of a fat turkey, only longer. He is covered in feathers and has a pointy snout. His sharp teeth shine. On each of

his back feet is a large round claw that is meant to tear open flesh.

Mike doesn't move. He stares at me. His head is tilted to the side like he is thinking.

A hundred questions run through my brain. They all try to come out at the same time. "Wha ... hun ... whe ... ?"

"I knew you'd like him," Mary says. She opens a cabinet on the wall and pulls out a box of dog treats.

"Where did you get him?" I ask.

"Mommy and Daddy found him before I was born. He is from All-Straw-La."

"Do you mean Australia?" I ask.

"That is what I said," Mary replies.

"Is he friendly?" I ask. Mike still hasn't moved. I don't think he has even blinked.

"He's the nicest dinosaur in the whole wide world." Mary gives him a dog treat and a hug around the neck.

Mike makes a rumbly noise. I think it's a happy noise. I hope it is, because this dinosaur has razor-sharp teeth and claws that could slice us open.

"What does he eat?" I ask. "Other than dog treats?" I know *Velociraptors* ate small animals. I'm not small, but my fingers are.

"He likes hamburgers," Mary says.

Suddenly, Mike lifts his head like he hears something. Saurus does the same thing when we open a can of cat food.

"Mary?" Mr. Stark calls from outside the trailer. "Mary?"

"Uh-oh," Mary says. "I'm not supposed to visit Mike without Mommy or Daddy. Quick. Hide."

The trailer doesn't have a lot of places to hide. There is a doghouse in the corner. I guess it's a dino house. It's plastic and shaped like an igloo.

"In there!" I point to the dino house.

Mary and I crawl inside. Mike's red and blue feathers cover the floor.

The door to the trailer opens. Mike runs in circles like an excited puppy.

"Mary?" Mr. Stark calls.

I hold my breath. Mostly because I don't want to get caught. Also, because it's stinky in the dino house.

Mr. Stark doesn't come inside the trailer. He closes the door and calls Mary's name again.

Mary and I tumble out of the dino house. Mike rushes over and checks me out. He nudges me with his nose and licks my ear. I hope I don't taste like food.

"You better go to your dad," I say to Mary. "He will get worried if he can't find you."

"Okay," Mary says. "Will you come over and play with Mike and me again?"

"Definitely!"

"Don't tell anyone about Mike. Remember, you promised." Mary holds up her pinky finger.

"I won't." I cross my heart.

"Last time I showed Mike to a friend, Mommy and Daddy made us leave the next day. I don't want to leave again."

"I don't want you to leave either."

Slash or Big V

When I walk into the house, Peanut jumps onto me. Gram and PopPop are in the living room. They're not smiling.

"Where have you been?" PopPop asks.

"You can't leave Peanut alone," Gram adds. "He chewed up a kitchen chair. He ate it like it was a stalk of celery."

I can't answer PopPop's question because Peanut is going nuts. He sniffs my clothes, my shoes, and my hair. He scratches at my shirt. He snorts when he smells my ear.

"It's okay, Peanut." I set him down, and he attacks my shoelaces.

"What is wrong with him?" PopPop asks.

"He smells something he doesn't like. Dinosaurs have a much better sense of smell than us." Gram puts her hands on her hips. "Would you like to explain?"

Sam runs into the room. She shoves her plastic microphone in my face. "Frank Mudd, are you hiding something from your grandparents?"

I push the microphone away. I told Mary I wouldn't tell anyone about Mike. She made me pinky promise. I don't know what to do.

It feels like I stand there for an hour waiting for my brain to come up with an idea.

"Frank?" Gram says.

I crack under the pressure.

"The Starks have a dinosaur!" I yell. "A *Velociraptor*!"

I expected everyone to scream and get excited. Instead, they just stare at me.

"He's about this big." I hold out my arms. "He has red and blue feathers. He eats dog treats. And they call him Mike." Which isn't a very good name for a dinosaur. I would have named him Slash or Big V.

PopPop looks at Gram. She shakes her head.

"It's not possible," she mumbles. But I can tell she believes me a little.

"Well, Mike wouldn't be the first." PopPop shrugs.

"Actually, he would," I say. "He's older than Peanut. Mike is at least five."

"And where do they keep this red-and-blue dinosaur?" Sam asks into her microphone.

"In a trailer," I say. "It's got a horse painted on the side. Probably to fool people."

"You mean *that* trailer?" Sam points out the front door. "The one driving away?"

I run out onto the porch. The Starks' Jeep pulls the trailer down the street. A cloud of brown dust follows.

"Oh no! They're leaving. Mary said this would happen if I told anyone. But I didn't expect it to be this quick." I pull on Gram's sleeve. "Get the truck. We can still catch them."

"Hold your dinosaurs, Frank." PopPop grabs

my shoulders and spins me around. "That's the Starks' RV right there. They didn't leave."

PopPop is right. The RV is still in the DECoW parking lot.

"Maybe we should go talk to the Starks," Gram says. "Clear up all this *Velociraptor* business."

"Or," I say, "maybe you could just believe me and not say anything. That way Mary won't get in trouble. You don't want to get Mary in trouble, do you?"

Sam and I follow Gram and PopPop to the RV. I guess they're not worried about getting Mary in trouble.

PopPop is about to knock on the Starks' door when it swings open.

"Hi there," Mrs. Stark says with a big smile. "I'm almost done with lunch and ready to get back to that fossil."

"Us too," Gram says.

"And let me thank you again for letting us

set up here," Mrs. Stark says. "I hope it's not too much trouble."

"No trouble at all," PopPop says.

"Where is the horse trailer?" Gram asks.

Mrs. Stark keeps smiling. "Neil and Mary took it into town. It needs some repairs."

"What do you keep in there?" Gram asks.

"Equipment," Mrs. Stark says quickly.

"Frank said he saw a *Velociraptor* in your trailer," Sam says.

"A *Velociraptor*?" Mrs. Stark says.

"Yeah," Sam says. "It's a kind of dinosaur."

Mrs. Stark laughs. "I know what a *Velociraptor* is, Sam. I just don't know why Frank would think we have one."

"Because I saw it." My voice wobbles.

"Okay," Mrs. Stark says. "We have a little secret. We have a pet we didn't tell you about because he makes some people a bit nervous. We have an Andean condor."

"That is a type of bird. A vulture," Gram says. "You have a pet vulture?"

"His name is Mike," Mrs. Stark says. "We found him years ago. He was injured and we took him in. Mary thinks he's a dinosaur. Sorry if she confused you, Frank."

For a second, I wonder if I was wrong. Is Mike really an Andean condor? No way. I know a dinosaur when I see one. I'm an expert. But I need to see him one more time just to make sure.

Playing Construction Site

I **secretly borrow Gram's** laptop to look up the Andean condor. The minute I see a picture, I know that is not the animal I saw in the Starks' trailer. Mike is bigger than this bird. He is also more colorful and has longer legs and sharp teeth. I have never seen a *Velociraptor* before. But I'm sure I saw one today.

The next day, all us humans, except PopPop, head to the dig site. Peanut stays in his pen in

FILE Edit VIEW HISTORY

Andean Condor

ANDEAN CONDOR

the garage. He doesn't like it. He growls and moans when I leave him.

At the site, Mr. Stark has one camera set up on the edge of the pit. He carries another camera on his shoulder. Mrs. Stark runs wires to a computer.

Sam instantly forgets that the fossil is the star of the show, not her.

"This is Sam McCarthy, reporting live from Wyoming." She holds her plastic microphone.

"It's not live," I point out.

"The cameras aren't even on yet," Aaron adds. We called him last night and told him all about the Starks and their documentary. I think Aaron is excited—I've never seen him with combed hair before.

"Hey, Frank!" Sam yells. "Look, a dinosaur!" She points to a couple of hawks flying around. She laughs so hard, she almost falls into the pit.

"What is so funny?" Aaron asks.

"Dino expert Frank Mudd can't even tell a bird from a dinosaur," Sam says. She thinks this is super funny. I don't.

"The Starks have a dinosaur," I say. "And I'm going to prove it. I just need to find the trailer." Mr. Stark and Mary drove back to DECoW last night but without the trailer. I don't believe Mrs. Stark's story that it needs to be fixed.

"And how are you going to find the trailer?" Sam asks. "This is Wyoming. It's a big place."

"Well, there's someone who knows where the trailer is," I say.

"Mr. and Mrs. Stark aren't going to tell you where they're hiding their bird," Sam says.

I shake my head. "I'm talking about Mary."

We can't see Mary, but we can hear her. She's singing on the other side of the dig. We find her playing with some old toy trucks.

"Hi," she says when we walk over. "I'm playing construction site. Do you want to play with me?"

"I love playing construction site." Aaron plops down next to her. He picks up a cement truck from the pile.

"Mary," Sam says, "is there really a dinosaur in your trailer?"

Mary smiles at me and holds up her pinky to remind me of the promise.

"You can trust them, Mary," I say. "They're bad at following rules. But good at keeping secrets."

Sam leans over Mary and gives her the evil eye. "Tell us, kid!"

Mary laughs. Sam is trying to be scary. Mary just thinks we're all very funny.

"Do you know where the trailer is?" I ask.

Mary nods. But then we're interrupted.

"What is going on here?" Mrs. Stark walks up behind us. "Mary?"

"Hi, Mommy," Mary says. "I'm playing construction site."

"Good." Mrs. Stark looks at me. "Mary needs to play alone today, kids. She is in a time-out."

"A really, really, really, really long one," Mary says.

I want to ask why, but I think I already know the answer.

As we start walking away, Mary pulls on my sock. I stop. She hands me a folded note and says, "Shhh."

I hide the note in my pocket just in time. Mrs. Stark turns around and gives me a long, scary stare.

"Frank," she says. "I hope you know how important this project is to us and to DECoW."

I nod.

"Good. Now let's focus on the fossils and not worry about any stories Mary may have told you. Got it?" Mrs. Stark says.

"Got it." I try to walk away, but she steps in front of me.

"I'm serious." Mrs. Stark sounds like a mean substitute teacher. "If I hear any more talk about raptors, we are leaving."

I swallow the lump in my throat. Mrs. Stark is scarier than a meat-eating dinosaur.

The Great Wall of China in Wyoming

At lunchtime, Sam and I go back to the house to check on Peanut. I think the Starks were happy to see us go because Sam kept *accidentally* stepping in front of the camera.

We take Peanut into the backyard so he can do his business. That means go poop and pee. I get the lettuce, grass, and twig mix from the fridge. Gram makes this special for him. We call it Peanut's salad.

There are no grown-ups around, so I can finally read Mary's note.

"What is that?" Sam asks.

"It's from Mary." The note isn't really a note. It doesn't have words, only a picture.

Sam steals the paper from me. "Mary isn't really an artist."

"She's a great artist," I sort of lie. "I know exactly what this is."

"What?" she asks.

"Well, that is the dinosaur." I point to Mike.

"You mean *bird*." Sam laughs.

I ignore her. "And that is a tree. There is a cloud. And that is the Great Wall of China."

"So it's in China?" Sam shakes her head. "This isn't very helpful."

The Great Wall of China? That didn't make sense. Then the answer pops into my brain.

"I got it!" I shout. "That isn't the Great Wall. It's a fence."

"But which fence?" Sam asks.

There are a lot of fences around here. Most of them are made of wire. I know of only one made of stone.

"This must be the stone fence around the old house," I say.

"Awesome!" Sam's eyes get big. I worry they might fall out of her head.

The old house is on the corner of Gram and PopPop's land. Actually, it *was* on the corner of their land. PopPop was born in the house, but it burned down a long time ago. The only thing left is the stone chimney, two wells, and the stone fence.

"We have to go," Sam says.

"We can't. We're not allowed, and it's dangerous." Both are very good reasons.

"What is so dangerous?" Sam asks.

"You could fall in a well. The chimney could collapse and crush you." I try to think of another reason. "You could get bitten by a rattlesnake or a mosquito."

"Why do you keep saying *you*?" she asks.

"Huh?"

"You should say *we* could fall in a well and die. *We* could get crushed by the chimney and die. *We* could get bitten by a snake and die." She grabs my hand like we are a crime-fighting duo.

"I never said die."

"You were thinking it," she says. "I'm going to the old house to find that condor or whatever it is. You can come with me, or you can stay here. I'll give you a full report when I get back." She pulls out her microphone. Sam loves to give full reports.

"Fine, I'll go with you," I say.

We wait for Peanut to finish his lunch. We decide to take him with us because it wouldn't be nice to lock him up all afternoon.

The old house is about two miles away, down

an old dirt road. We fill our backpacks. Sam's has supplies like water, snacks, and her microphone. Mine has Peanut.

Peanut tumbles around in the bag.

"Be good!" I yell at the bouncing backpack. "Or I'll leave you at home."

We get our bikes out of the garage. We're just about to leave when Saurus jumps in front of my bike.

She meows super loud.

"What is it?" I ask.

"You don't expect her to answer, do you?" Sam raises her eyebrows.

"No." But I wish she would. She's either saying "Take me with you" or "Don't go, because you'll get hurt."

I pick up Saurus and put her in the basket on the front of my bike. I think she actually shakes her head no. But she doesn't jump out.

"Let's go!" Sam races down the road. She's faster than me, but she isn't carrying a cat and a grumpy dinosaur.

Sam makes a turn at the Crabtrees' ranch. I guess she thinks we need to bring Aaron too.

Soon all three of us are riding toward the old house. My bike jerks and skids over the rough road. It's kind of fun. I even jump a pothole.

"There it is!" Sam shouts. We can see the old chimney in the distance. And behind it is the Starks' horse trailer.

A few raindrops land on my face. Dark clouds hide the sun. I definitely don't want to be out here in a storm.

"It's raining," I say. I stop my bike in front of Sam's. "Maybe we should come back with Gram and PopPop."

"This is nothing," Aaron says. "Wait until we get a really big storm with thunder and lightning. I've seen the wind rip the roof off a barn."

"What are you so scared of?" Sam says.

"I'm not scared." I bike ahead of her. I just don't want to be eaten by a dinosaur.

Dino Senses Are Tingling

We lean our bikes against a tree.

"So this is PopPop's old house," Sam says. "I've never been here." She climbs over the stone fence.

"Be careful," I say. Rattlesnakes like to hide in the scraggly bushes that are everywhere. And the old wells are perfect for kids, cats, or dinosaurs to fall into.

"Is the dinosaur in there?" Aaron points at the trailer.

I nod. "Maybe I should go first. I've met Mike before, so he probably won't eat me."

"No way," Sam says. "I'm going first." She sprints through the front yard and past the chimney. Aaron is right behind her.

I grab Peanut. Saurus takes a step back. She's a smart cat.

"Wait for me." I race after them.

Sam gets to the door of the trailer first. She twists the handle.

"He's a carnivore," I warn her. "He may be hungry."

"It's locked," she says.

"I got this." Aaron picks up a rock the size of a soccer ball.

"No!" I shout. I point at the ground where Aaron's rock had been. "Let's just use the key. The Starks must have hidden it here."

Sam unlocks the door and pulls it open. Inside, it's super quiet. And dark.

"Mike?" I step in. "It's me, Frank. We met yesterday." I walk slowly toward Mike's igloo. Sam and Aaron follow.

Mike pokes his head out. And I'm one thousand percent sure he is not a bird.

"Wha . . ." Sam can't talk, which doesn't happen a lot.

"Meet Mike," I say.

"What is it?" Aaron asks.

"He's a *Velociraptor,*" I answer.

"But he has feathers," Aaron says.

"Lots of dinosaurs had feathers," I explain. "That doesn't make them birds. And it doesn't mean they could fly." It feels good to be right.

Peanut fights to get out of my arms. He

whines and makes a clicking noise in his throat. I'm not sure if he wants to meet Mike or have a battle. It would be the first dinosaur fight in sixty-five million years.

Mike doesn't like the sound. He inches back into his igloo. We can't see him anymore.

"Hold Peanut." I hand him to Sam. Then I get down on my hands and knees and look inside the igloo. There is a small chance Mike will jump out and attack my face. But my dino senses are telling me he's more scared than I am.

Mike is curled up. His long snout is tucked under his feathery arms. I can't see his killer claws.

"It's okay, Mike. We're all friends." I wave to him.

Mike doesn't move.

"What did you bring for snacks?" I ask Sam.

"Cookies and potato chips. A couple of apples and some spinach for Peanut," she says.

"Nothing a carnivore can eat," I say.

"I have some buffalo jerky." Aaron reaches into the pocket of his shorts. "It's barbecue flavor."

I take a piece of jerky from Aaron and hold it out to Mike. "Come on, buddy."

Slowly, Mike crawls toward the meat. I move back a little. If he wants it, he's going to have to come out of his dino house.

Peanut whines and twists in Sam's arms.

When Mike is all the way out, I let him have the treat.

"Good boy," I say. Carefully, I reach out to pat his head. He sniffs my fingers before letting me touch him.

"Where did he come from?" Sam asks. "Did he hatch from an egg too?"

"I don't know. Mary said her parents have had him since before she was born."

"You guys have a dinosaur," Aaron says. "And Mary has a dinosaur. It's not fair. I want one. I call dibs on the next dinosaur we find."

"Fine. You get the next dinosaur." Sam rolls her eyes.

I feel bad for Mike. If Mary hadn't shown him

to me, maybe he would still be with his family and not out here all alone.

I give him another piece of jerky.

"We have to tell Gram and PopPop," Sam says. "I bet they'll adopt Mike."

"I already tried to tell them once," I remind her. "They didn't believe me."

Sam nods. "They believed you until Mrs. Stark lied. I knew grown-ups lied. I'll never trust another one."

"Maybe we should wait to tell Gram and Pop-Pop," I suggest.

"Why?" Aaron asks.

"If we tell them, you know they'll say something to the Starks," I explain. "And then the Starks will leave. That means no documentary."

Sam gasps. "No!"

"And no money for Peanut's new house," I add.

I give Sam and Aaron a minute to think about

it. That might be the longest they've thought about anything all summer.

"We'll wait and tell Gram and PopPop after the documentary is done. Agreed?" I ask.

We all put our hands in. "Agreed."

Hanging Out with a Carnivore

I have to wait a whole day before I can sneak off again to see Mike. Sam and Aaron have soccer practice. I should be there too, but I pretend that Peanut ate my shin guards. PopPop is running DECoW. Gram and the Starks are digging up fossils and filming it.

This time I pack more supplies, like my notebook, a scale and tape measure, and meat. Peanut comes along. I think he's worried I might like Mike more than him. That would never happen.

I ride my bike to the old house and trailer. The key is right where we left it.

"Hi, Mike," I say as I open the door. "It's me, Frank. And Peanut."

Mike meets us at the door. Actually, he tries to run through the door. I drop Peanut and tackle Mike before he can escape.

"You have to stay here. Mary would miss you if you ran away." I pet his head. He seems to relax. Until he sees Peanut sniffing around his dino house.

Mike squawks. He lifts his arms and fans his feathers out like a peacock.

Peanut yelps. Then he runs. But there is no place to really run in the trailer.

Mike chases Peanut. I chase Mike. We go in circles like we're playing duck, duck, dinosaur.

"Stop, dinosaurs. Stop right now!" I yell. They

don't listen. So we keep running until I can't run anymore. If I had wanted exercise, I would have gone to soccer.

Finally, I give up. I plop down on the floor and try to catch my breath. Peanut jumps into my lap. And then so does Mike.

My lap isn't big enough for two dinosaurs. I push them off. Peanut bites Mike's tail. They start chasing each other again. This time, Peanut is It.

"I'll just wait until you're done playing." As

they run laps around me, I take out the scale, tape measure, and notebook.

I'm not really worried that Mike will eat Peanut. Mike is a carnivore, but I bet the Starks have been feeding him carrion. Carrion is dead meat. Mike doesn't know how to hunt. And the Starks have trimmed the killer claws on his back feet.

I write all of this in my notebook.

When Mike and Peanut finally tire out, I give them a snack. Mike gets lunch meat. Peanut gets carrots.

"Time for your physical, Mike." I gently lead him onto the scale by dangling another piece of meat. He puts only one leg on the scale, so I have to guess his weight. I write down *Twenty-five pounds.*

Getting his height and length are just as hard. He likes to bite the tape measure. *Two or three feet tall. Three or four or five feet long.*

I also want to count his teeth, but after he bites the tape measure in half, I decide to estimate the number of teeth. *Teeth: a lot. And sharp.*

While I write up my notes, Peanut and Mike play chase again. Then they wrestle. And then they curl up together for a nap.

I watch the two dinosaurs sleep and think I'm the luckiest kid in the world. Until I look at my watch.

"Peanut! We need to go." Soccer practice ended thirty minutes ago, and DECoW closes soon.

Peanut jumps at my feet. I pick him up. Mike whines and circles us.

"Sorry, Mike. We'll be back. I promise." I smooth the feathers on his head and give him the last slice of lunch meat.

Peanut and I rush out of the trailer. We get on my bike and ride to the house. We try to sneak in through the back door. Gram spots us right away.

"Frank, there you are. You won't believe—"

"Hey, Gram! How's it going? I've had a really, really boring day! Nothing exciting happened here! Nothing at all!"

"Frank, stop yelling," Gram says.

"Sorry."

Then Gram gives me a big smile. "Well, I *did* have an exciting day. We found another fossil today. This one is much smaller. Almost Peanut's size." She takes him from me and rubs a spot under his chin. "I think it's safe to say that this little guy is a pack animal."

"Yeah. I already knew that." I want to tell her that he even likes hanging out with carnivores, but I keep that to myself.

Sam Did It

The Starks are already at the site when Gram, Sam, and I get there the next morning. Mr. and Mrs. Stark are setting up. Mary plays in the dirt.

Sam whips out her plastic microphone. "Testing. Testing. I'm ready for my first scene." She dashes out of the truck and goes right to Mrs. Stark.

"Where's the new fossil?" I ask Gram.

"Where all the cameras are pointing," she

says. There are only two cameras, but they are both aimed at the same spot.

I hop carefully into the pit. Only part of the fossil has been cleared. There could be a lot more in the rock.

"That is a rib, right?" I ask Gram.

She nods. "I believe so."

"And this is the base of the skull." I point with my finger.

"Yes, and that tip right there—"

"Is the peanut-shaped horn," I say. It's amazing.

Mr. Stark walks over. "Good morning, Frank. Glad you're back on site today. We missed you yesterday." I wonder if he's saying one thing but means something else. Grown-ups do that sometimes.

"Dr. Mudd, we'd like to get your opinion on some of yesterday's video." He points to Mrs. Stark and the computer.

"I'd love to," Gram says. And she is definitely saying one thing but means something else.

I pick up a brush and start clearing away some of the rock around the fossil. Sam jumps down beside me.

"Mrs. Stark says she doesn't need me in the scene today. Can you believe that?" Sam asks.

"Maybe they'll need you later." I just say it to make her feel better.

"What are you digging at?" Sam doesn't offer to help.

"It's another fossil," I say. "It's like the big fossil Gram found, but smaller." I don't mention Peanut on purpose. The Starks could overhear.

"That's cool, I guess." Sam leans back against the wall of the pit.

"You guess? Of course it's cool. All fossils are cool. They're more than cool. They're awesome!" I shout.

"Okay." Sam shrugs. "I just don't see how you

can get so excited about a fossil when you have a real dinosaur waiting for you in the garage."

"Shhh! Someone might hear you." I turn my back to Sam and brush the fossil. She just doesn't get it.

"Whatever," she says.

"Why don't you go jump in front of a camera again?" I suggest.

"I *am* in front of a camera," she snaps back. "And look. That one is on!"

Huh?

I stand up. One of the cameras has a glowing red light. *It is on!*

"Sam." I pull her up and whisper into her ear, "You just said stuff in front of the camera you weren't supposed to say."

"What? About Peanut being in the garage?" She slaps a hand over her mouth.

I scramble out of the pit, pulling Sam with me. "Come on. You have to help me erase it."

I hit a button. The red light goes out. Good. That's step one.

"Hey, what are you doing with that camera?" Mr. Stark yells from the far side of the pit.

"Quick, erase it." I push Sam into the camera stand.

She presses every button. She flicks every switch. I don't think she knows what she's doing.

"I'm better in *front* of the camera," she says.

"Don't touch the equipment," Mrs. Stark says in her scary-substitute-teacher voice. The grown-ups are running toward us.

There's no time. I yank the camera off its stand. I was going to run away with it, but Sam grabs it from me. She throws it into the pit.

"No!" screams Mr. Stark.

Everyone stops. The camera is still in one piece. I kind of expected it to blow up like a bomb.

"You're in trouble. You're in trouble," Mary sings.

Mrs. Stark picks up the camera and plays with it for a minute. "The lens is shattered. The circuits are shot."

I let out a big breath.

"Yes!" Sam says. She tries to give me a high five, but I don't move.

"What has gotten into you two?" Gram is standing in front of us. Sam and I just stare at our feet.

"Get in the truck. You are done here."

P-E-A-N-U-T

The Starks make some phone calls and find a place that can fix their camera. The repair shop is over an hour away. Mary doesn't want to go, so PopPop suggests she stay with us.

"It's the least we can do," he says.

"Yeah!" Mary exclaims. "Can I meet your dinosaur now?"

"I don't have a dinosaur," I say. Again!

Mary, Sam, and I watch TV and play Memory Match. We can't go outside because of the rain.

PopPop works the front desk at DECoW, and Gram goes to the dig site. She wants to cover the fossils with a tarp to protect them from the weather. I'm not allowed back there. Maybe not ever.

I set up another board game. We hear thunder. It sounds far away.

"I don't like thunderstorms," Mary says.

"It'll be okay," Sam says. "We're safe in the house."

Mary nods. She's okay until there is another boom of thunder.

"What about Mike?" she asks. "Will he be safe too?"

Through the front window, we see black clouds over the hills.

"He'll be fine," Sam says.

"Mike is all alone," Mary says. "And he hates thunder too."

I bring Mary into the kitchen and pour her a glass of chocolate milk. She doesn't drink it.

"I'm going to check on P-E-A-N-U-T." I spell out his name so Mary won't know who I'm talking about.

Peanut has been quiet all morning. I should have known something was up. He broke free from the pen in the garage and found a box of Halloween decorations to play with. Pieces of a plastic pumpkin are everywhere.

I give him a carrot and try to clean up some of the mess.

"For a small dinosaur, you are a lot of work." I fix the hole in his pen and put him back in it.

When I return to the kitchen, Mary is alone.

"Where's Sam?" I ask.

"She went to get Mike." Mary smiles.

"What?" I run to the window. I don't see Sam, only lightning flashing behind DECoW.

"She took her bike," Mary says. "She's going to rescue Mike. Then Mommy and Daddy won't be so mad about the broken camera."

Rain taps on the side of the house. A crash of thunder makes the walls shake and the lights blink. A second later, there is scratching at the door to the garage.

Mary gets up from her chair. Before I can stop her, she pulls it open.

Peanut runs into the room and jumps into my arms.

"I knew it," Mary squeals. "I knew you had a dinosaur!" She pats Peanut gently on the top of his head.

"This is Peanut," I say.

Another crash of thunder booms. Both Peanut and Mary jump.

"We better help Sam," I say. "Come on."

I take Mary's hand and shove Peanut under my shirt. We run across the parking lot to DECoW. We get soaked.

"What are you doing out in this weather?" PopPop takes off his glasses and rubs his eyes.

"Sam is gone. She went to the old house," I explain.

"What? Why?" PopPop is on his feet.

"She went to rescue my rapper," Mary says.

"It's a long story," I say.

"We don't have time," PopPop says. "This is a bad storm. Let's go." He yells for one of the workers to lock up.

Saurus is waiting for us under the car. Somehow she's not even wet.

PopPop can't drive fast. The rain hits the

windshield so hard it's like we're going through the car wash.

"What was that girl thinking?" PopPop mumbles.

"She's trying to do the right thing." I don't usually stand up for Sam. I hope PopPop and Mary don't tell her.

When another flash lights the sky, I can see the old chimney in the distance. Peanut must sense we are getting close. He starts his cry that sounds like a violin.

The road is filling with water. PopPop drives around a puddle as big as a pond. The car slips. Then stops. Then it feels like we're sinking.

"Rats!" PopPop exclaims. "We're stuck in the mud." The car spins and groans, but it doesn't go forward.

"Let's get Sam and Mike, and then we can get unstuck," I say. Not that I know how to *unstuck* a car.

"Who is Mike?" PopPop asks.

"My rapper," Mary says.

I open the door and jump out. The rain has let up a little, or maybe I'm so wet that I can't tell anymore.

As I run to the trailer, I look back over my shoulder. PopPop, Mary, and Peanut are right behind me. Saurus stays in the car and watches us.

Peanut catches up. He is definitely smiling. He likes adventure.

We splash through the yard filled with puddles. A big wind pushes us faster. The trailer rocks. Sam's bike falls over.

"Sam!" I shout.

"Mikey!" Mary yells.

Lightning strikes a tree at the end of the yard. The tree cracks in half. Sparks fly.

Just as we get to the trailer, the door opens. Sam is holding a shaking Mike in her arms.

PopPop comes to a stop like he ran into a glass wall. "Is that . . ."

"It's a *Velociraptor*," I say, but there's no time to explain.

Sam jumps out of the trailer. Mike leaps from her arms. He goes to Mary first. She gives him a crushing hug. Then Mike tackles Peanut, which I think is his way of saying hello.

"It's not safe out here," PopPop says. "We need to get home."

"We better hurry!" Sam yells. "Look!" She points down the road. It's a tornado!

Stinky Storm Shelter

My **mouth drops** open. I've never seen a tornado in real life. It's scarier than a monster movie.

"There's an old underground storm shelter around here. I remember from when I was a boy," PopPop says. He starts counting his steps at the corner of the stone fence.

The tornado is getting closer. It sounds like a big rig truck driving straight at us.

"Hurry, PopPop," Sam says.

"Thirty-two. Thirty-three. Here!" He kicks something metal with his foot. Then he bends down to lift a handle. Mud and bushes cover the shelter door.

"Help me, kids." We all start digging.

PopPop tries to lift the handle again. The door opens.

"Quick, down the ladder." PopPop holds the door open.

There isn't any light in the storm shelter, and it kind of smells like a bathroom. I don't want to go into the scary hole.

But then I look up and see the tornado. I'm the first to climb down. If there is a monster in here, it doesn't attack. I help Mary down the ladder. Sam hands me the dinosaurs one at a time. She and Pop-Pop come in last. The door bangs shut behind them.

"Saurus!" I yell. I try to scramble back up the ladder, but a hand stops me.

"You can't go out there," PopPop says.

Something brushes against my leg. I hope it's a dinosaur and not something scary.

A small light appears. It's PopPop's cell phone.

"Can't make a call, but it works as a flashlight," he says.

I look around the shelter. It's the size of a big closet. There is a high shelf with some dusty cans on it and two metal benches. And on one of the benches is my cat.

"Saurus! How did you get here?" I pick her up. "And how are you not wet?"

"Well, we're all safe," PopPop says. "Now we just have to wait out the storm."

We sit on the benches. PopPop turns off his phone to save the battery. I hold Saurus in one arm and Peanut in the other. I want to keep them close in case Mike gets hungry.

"If someone had told me when I was a boy that I'd return to this musty storm shelter with my grandkids, their friend, a cat, and two dinosaurs . . . well, I never would have believed him." PopPop laughs.

"How will we know when the storm is over?" I ask.

"Oh, you'll know. Just listen," PopPop says.

So I do. I hear the big rig again. I know it's not actually a truck. It's the tornado.

It gets louder. The door bounces a little and bits of light pop in. I liked it better when it was dark.

The shelter shakes. The big rig sounds like a train now. It's just missing the whistle.

"It's almost over!" PopPop yells.

Sam grabs my hand. I close my eyes. Maybe a tornado is what made the dinosaurs go extinct the first time.

"Count to one hundred," PopPop says. "Then it'll be over. That's what I used to do when I was a boy."

"I can count to a thousand," Mary says.

"You won't need to, sweetheart," PopPop says to her.

Sam, Mary, and I count together. The train seems to drive away. By the time we hit fifty, it's all quiet. The door has stopped rattling.

PopPop gets up to check it out. He flings open the door. The sunlight hurts my eyes.

"What a beautiful day," he says, and smiles.

We climb out of the shelter. To the west, the sky is sunny and blue. The end of the storm moves away from us.

"Look at the trailer," Sam says. It has been knocked on its side.

"Good thing we got Mike out," I say.

The car is still stuck in the mud. PopPop's cell phone doesn't have a signal. So we walk the two miles home.

A Big Fence

Gram and **Mr.** and Mrs. Stark are waiting for us on the front porch. We must look pretty weird walking up the dirt road. Three kids, two dinosaurs, one cat, and PopPop.

They run out to meet us.

"That is a *Velociraptor*!" Gram yells. She pulls Sam and me behind her. I think she's trying to protect us.

"I know." I smile.

Gram looks at Mrs. Stark. "That is *not* an Andean condor."

Mrs. Stark picks up Mary and hugs her tight. Then she points at Peanut. "And what is that?"

Mr. Stark gets down on his knees and looks closely at Peanut.

"He's a *Wyomingasaurus,*" Sam says.

"Hot dog!" Gram stares at Mike. "I can't believe this."

"Me neither," Mr. Stark says.

"Maybe we should talk about this in the house," PopPop says. "It's been an exciting afternoon."

We all sit in the living room. Gram gives Peanut a salad and Mike an uncooked hamburger.

"I guess I broke the camera for nothing," Sam says.

Gram shakes her head.

"Where did Mike come from?" PopPop asks.

"He found us in Perth, Australia," Mrs. Stark

explains. "It was almost ten years ago. We were filming one of our first documentaries. Mike just walked into our camp. We gave him some of our dinner, and he became part of the family."

"He didn't hatch from an egg?" Sam asks.

"He may have," Mrs. Stark says. "But we don't know when or where. We've been traveling the globe searching for more *Velociraptors* and other dinosaurs. Peanut is the first one we've met."

"Awesome," I say. "That's what I want to do when I grow up. Travel the world looking for extinct animals."

"You're off to a good start," Mrs. Stark says.

"So you found another dinosaur," Sam says. "Our dinosaur. Now what?"

"Can we keep him?" Mary asks.

"No!" Gram and I answer.

Mary makes a sad face. It doesn't last long because Peanut jumps in her lap.

"What's your plan for Peanut?" Mr. Stark asks.

"We'll build him a home here," Gram says. "Our neighbors are donating land, and so are we. We need to make Peanut a safe place to roam."

"We're going to need a big fence," I add.

"Perhaps we could find room for Mike. If you're interested." Gram scratches the *Velociraptor* under the chin.

"We're not interested," Mrs. Stark says.

I guess no one wants to give up a dinosaur.

"You're going to finish the documentary, right?" Sam asks. She puts her hands together and begs for the right answer.

Mr. and Mrs. Stark look at each other.

"We were talking about that," Mr. Stark says. "And we think we want to do a shorter documentary. Like a twenty-minute show for a website. Something for kids. Sam, would you like to narrate for us?"

"Yes!" She whips out her plastic microphone faster than I've ever seen.

Meet Joe

The Starks promise to keep Peanut a secret from the rest of the world. And we agree to keep Mike a secret. At least until they each have a safe and happy habitat. I'm worried that without a big, long documentary, DECoW won't have enough money to build Peanut's home. But Gram tells me that is something for grown-ups to worry about, not me.

The next week goes by super quick. It might

be the most fun week of my life. We spend the days digging out the *Wyomingasaurus* fossils. We spend the evenings having cookouts and letting our dinosaurs play together. Chase is their favorite game. Mary and I would rather play dinosaur trivia. She knows a lot, but I always win. Except when I let her win.

Today, Mr. Stark, PopPop, and I sort the new fossils in the DECoW lab. It's like putting a giant puzzle together. We take a break when the camera repair guy shows up.

"It's all fixed," Joe the repair guy says. He has a name tag pinned to his shirt. He's skinny and tall but looks more like a kid than a grown-up.

"We recovered the footage too," he continues. "It's all there."

A lump grows in my throat. I swallow it down. I remember what was on the camera. Why we broke it in the first place. No one would believe Sam's story about a real dinosaur in a garage. Would they?

"Great," Mr. Stark says. "And thanks for delivering it. I thought I would have to pick it up."

"No problem." Joe smiles. "I wanted to see DECoW. I've lived in Wyoming my whole life and have never been here. This place is cool."

"Take a look around," PopPop says, and then he gives Joe a free ticket.

"Thank you, sir." Joe walks into the museum.

PopPop turns to Mr. Stark. "How much do we owe you?"

"Don't worry about it," Mr. Stark says. "We appreciate you letting us stay here. And you saved Mike's life. I think we still owe you."

"Not at all," PopPop says. He pats Mr. Stark on the shoulder.

I don't feel like sorting fossils anymore. A worried feeling grows in my stomach. I want to talk to Sam and check on Peanut.

"I'll be back." I hang up my lab coat and leave.

As I walk across the parking lot, I can see Gram and PopPop's house. It looks dark and quiet. But then I notice someone crawling in the bushes.

A burglar!

My heart thumps.

I'm about to run back to DECoW for help when the person stands up. It's not a burglar. It's Joe, the camera repair guy. He's taking pictures through the window of the house.

He's taking pictures of Peanut!

"Hey!" I yell. "Stop!" I run toward him.

"Oh, hey." Joe waves at me. Then he takes off faster than a track star.

"Stop! Now!"

He doesn't. He jumps into his van. As he speeds by me, he shouts out the window, "Cool dinosaur!"

Dear Reader,

Sorry, that is all I can tell you right now. I have a problem that I need to take care of right away. You still need to keep this a secret. Please don't put this information on TV or in the newspaper or on the Internet. If you want to tell someone, tell your pet. Pets are good at keeping secrets. We need to keep Peanut safe.

Sincerely,
Frank Mudd

Glossary

Here are some words and definitions, in case you aren't a dinosaur expert like me.

Andean condor: not a dinosaur. It's a vulture that lives in South America.

carnivore: a meat-eating animal. Examples: *Velociraptor, T. rex,* tiger, shark.

carrion: dead meat. Some animals think carrion is yummy.

DECoW: Dinosaur Education Center of Wyoming. My grandparents own it.

fossil: proof of a living thing saved in rock. This can be footprints, bones, leaves, and more.

habitat: a natural home for an animal or plant. Peanut needs a big one.

herbivore: a plant-eating animal. Examples: Peanut, *Triceratops,* rabbit, some humans.

Ichthyosaur: not a dinosaur or a fish, but a reptile that lived in the ocean during dinosaur times.

Oviraptor: a birdlike dinosaur that watched over its nest of eggs.

paleontologist: a dinosaur scientist. Actually, paleontologists can study any kind of prehistoric life, not just dinos.

Supersaurus: a giant plant-eating dinosaur that lived near Wyoming (before it was Wyoming).

Velociraptor: a smallish dinosaur that had feathers and walked on two legs. Its name means "speedy thief."

Wyomingasaurus: a new species of dinosaur. Peanut is one. We came up with the name—it's not official yet.

About the Author

Stacy McAnulty does not have a dinosaur. She does have three kids, two dogs, and one husband. She has been on a dinosaur dig in Wyoming, where she found a small fossil. It wasn't an egg. Stacy grew up in upstate New York but now calls North Carolina home. (She still really wants a dinosaur—maybe an *Iguanodon*.) Learn more about The Dino Files at thedinofiles.com.

About the Illustrator

Mike Boldt loves ice cream, comics, and drawing. He is the illustrator of *I Don't Want to Be a Frog* and the author and illustrator of the forthcoming *A Tiger Tail*. Mike lives in Alberta, Canada, only a couple of hours from Drumheller, the site of that country's largest collection of dinosaur fossils.

Did Frank's dad find a dinosaur when he was a kid?

Turn the page for a sneak peek at the next Dino Files book!

A shaking wakes me up in the middle of the night. At first I think it's Peanut jumping on the bed. He does that sometimes.

"Frank, wake up." It's my dad. He is shaking me by the shoulders.

"I'm awake. I'm awake. What's wrong?" I ask. My pets are awake too. Peanut stands on my legs. Saurus stretches by my feet.

"I need to tell you something." Dad sits on

the edge of my bed. It's getting very crowded.

"What?"

"Or maybe I'll show you." Dad pops up and goes to the desk. It used to be his when he was a boy. The whole room used to be his. He pulls out the top drawer and flips it over. Pens and pencils fall to the floor. Peanut jumps up to see if there is anything good to eat.

A piece of paper is taped to the bottom of the drawer.

"Here." He unfolds it and hands it to me.

On the paper is a drawing. It looks like an eel but with four small legs. Written in the bottom corner is Dad's real name (Brian) and one word.

"*Nothosaurus,*" I read.

"Yes!" Dad says. "That's the creature I found when I was a boy." He taps the paper.

"Really?" I ask.

"No way," Sam says. She walks into my room without knocking and takes the picture. "Is this the dinosaur you always wanted, Uncle Brian?"

"It's not a dinosaur," I say. "The *Nothosaurus* is a prehistoric reptile that lived in water."

Sam rolls her eyes. "Aren't dinosaurs prehistoric reptiles?"

"Yes, but not all prehistoric reptiles are dinosaurs," I say. "Just like cats are mammals. But that doesn't mean all mammals are cats. You're a mammal, and you're not a cat."

"It's basically a dinosaur," Sam shoots back. I

need to start a dinosaur school for her and other confused people.

"Do you want to hear my story?" Dad asks.

"Yes!" Sam and I both answer. We sit on my bed. Peanut curls up in her lap and Saurus in mine.

"I was twelve," Dad starts. "And I was canoeing on the river with three boys from scouts. We stopped to take a bathroom break."

"There are rest stops on the river?" Sam asks.

"Boys don't need an actual bathroom," I answer.

"Gross." She sticks out her tongue.

"I finished my business and got back first," Dad continues. "And there it was. A *Nothosaurus*. Sunning itself right next to our canoe."

"Did it attack you?" Sam asks.

"No. It just stared at me. The Notho was longer than our boat. It had purple-gray skin. No scales. And large black eyes." Dad scratches his beard. "What a sight. It wasn't afraid at all. At least not until the other boys came out of the woods. They were laughing and joking and being pretty loud."

"Did the *Nothosaurus* attack them?" Sam asks excitedly.

"No, Sam. It dove back into the river before the boys got a good look. One of them—a kid named Bart Matthews—saw part of the tail. He started screaming that it was a river monster. I tried to explain that it was a *Nothosaurus*. He didn't believe me. No one did."

"Not even Gram and PopPop?" I ask.

"I told them about it when I got home. They wanted to believe me," Dad says. "We went back to the river dozens of times. I never saw it again. As I grew older, I worried that I imagined the Notho."

"You didn't imagine it, Uncle Brian. If Peanut is real, I bet your river dinosaur is real too," Sam says.

"That's what I was thinking." Dad smiles.

"What about Bart Matthews?" I ask. "Did people believe him?"

"Bart always claimed it was a river monster. He drew a two-headed beast and told everyone in school that's what we found. So I drew my own picture. I didn't want to forget." Dad takes his paper back.

"Wait!" A thought hits my brain. "Is Bart the guy from the TV? Bart's River Monster Tours?"

"I've seen his commercials!" Sam yells. "My mom says he's crazy."

"That's him," Dad says.

"He's a friend of yours?" I ask.

"We aren't exactly friends," Dad explains. "I haven't seen him in twenty years. But tomorrow I think we should visit him."

New friends. New adventures.
Find a new series . . . just for you!

BALLPARK Mysteries
FOR THE SPORTS FAN

THE DINO Files
FOR THE ADVENTURER

Louise Trapeze
FOR THE SUPERSTAR

PIPER GREEN
FOR THE DREAMER

PUPPY PIRATES
FOR THE ANIMAL LOVER

Totally True adventures!
FOR THE EXPLORER

RandomHouseKids.com